I AM

What God Says I Am!

ESOURCE *Publications* • Eugene, Oregon

WRITTEN BY:
Shannon White

Resource Publications
A division of Wipf and Stock Publishers
199 W 8th Ave, Suite 3
Eugene, OR 97401

I Am What God Says I Am
By White, Shannon
Copyright©2015 by White, Shannon
ISBN 13: 978-1-5326-9199-7
Publication date 5/16/2019
Previously published by Tate Publishing, 2015

Dedicated to Kamari

Dedicado a Kamari

Acknowledgments

Big thanks to my pastors, parents, family, and husband for the encouragement! It makes the difference!

Big thanks to Paula Ospina for your translations! You are more than fabulous!

Big thanks to my sponsors—*HOPE for Women* magazine, Johnny White Jr., Robyn Morton, Rachel Gould, Kerry Gould, Joseph Morton, Debbi Rife, Terry Gould—and all other sponsors that have supported this endeavor!

Muchas gracias a mi pastor, padres, familia y esposo por el ánimo! Se siente/ nota la diferencia!

Muchas gracias a Paula Ospina por su traducción! Eres más que increíble!

Muchas gracias a mis patrocinadores, HOPE for Women magazine, Johnny White

Jr., Robyn Morton, Rachel Gould, Kerry Gould, Joseph Morton, Debbi Rife, Terry Gould y todos otros patrocinadores que el apoyo a esta iniciativa.

Note to Parents

Hello, children of God!

We live in a world that is invested in raising our next generation by giving them messages that are in conflict with the Bible about

- what to do,
- who they are,
- how to dress,
- how to talk,
- what is good and bad,
- who is God, and
- what they will be.

As a result, we have youth in distress—mentally, spiritually, emotionally, and physically—far more than when we were younger!

But what would happen if we took the kingdom back by force before it had a chance to get its grip on our young people?

Language acquisition begins in the third trimester of the womb. Completed studies suggest that the same words or sounds heard from the womb are embedded in the memory and activated in the baby's memory when recited again after birth! We sing songs and recite words to our babies in vitro, as well as in the earlier years of life, to teach them our language; and it is a fact that babies prefer their native language over other languages!

Let's think about it.

Samuel was in the temple from infancy and was well versed in the heavenly kingdom language, Moses was in Pharaoh's household from infancy and was well versed in their Egyptian kingdom language, and some babies have affinities to certain songs or words that were shared with them from infancy because it is familiar to them. But can you imagine what could happen if we began intentionally speaking the kingdom language and helping our babies learn kingdom language from their first years?

What power they could have at a young age!

As a school counselor and youth worker, I see the plight of our young people and the enemy's desires to sift them as wheat. I hear the negative things young people say about themselves as well as the internalization of the faulty messaging our society puts on them, and it breaks my heart. I wanted more for my son, as we all do as parents. As a new mother, I struggled with findings books that would meet my son's intellectual need for colors and literacy while satisfying his spiritual need for hearing the word of God proclaimed over his life. There were plenty of resources for me to read as a parent, but I could not find a book that I could recite with my son to stick into his memory for the church and the Holy Spirit to activate at the appropriate times in his life! For that reason I wrote this book.

This book is simply another tool we can use to pour God's word into the lives of our young people. As it is written, "Train up a child in the way that he should go; and when he is old he will not depart from it" (Proverbs 22:6, Kjv). Why not use our routine bedtime stories as a time to feed their spirit?

God also says, "So is my word that goes out from my mouth: It will not return to me empty, but will accomplish what I desires and achieve the purpose for which I sent it" (Isaiah 55:11, Niv).

We pour into our young people's lives with our daily language, and many people use the cliché that the power of a praying mother "got me through," but what would happen if our babies knew the promises God had for them and began speaking them as well?

Why wait until they are older? If they can say Da-da, Ma-ma, hey, and no, why can't they say Je (for Jesus) or God?

"For from the lips of children and infants you, Lord, have called forth your praise!" (Matthew 21:16b, Niv).

We must "Stay alert and watch out for your great enemy, the devil. He prowls around like a roaring lion looking for someone to devour" (1 Peter 5:8, Nlt). And this includes our babies. So while we plant seeds with the words we use—it is written that faith comes by hearing and hearing through the word of God (Romans 10:17, Esv)—why not kill two birds with one stone and allow the family-friendly time of reading to be also a spiritual-building time?

This book is just for that!

So enjoy and be encouraged even as we edify our babies!

English

*T*he earth is the Lord's and everything in it. The world and all its people belong to him! Including me! (Psalm 24:1, Nᴌᴛ)

Spanish

Del Señor es el mundo entero, con todo lo que en él hay, con todo lo que en él vive. (Salmo 24:1)

English

I am fearfully and wonderfully made! I am God's masterpiece so he knows my name! And the very hairs on my head are all numbered! (Psalm 139:14a, Ephesians 2:10a, Matthew 10:30; Nʟᴛ)

Spanish

Te alabo porque estoy maravillado, porque es maravilloso lo que has hecho. De ello estoy bien convencido! pues es Dios quien no has hecho; él nos ha creado en Cristo Jesús para que hagamos buenas obras, según él lo había dispuesto de antemano. En cuanto a ustedes mismos, hasta los cabellos de la cabeza los tienen contados uno por uno. (Salmo 139:14, Efesios 2:10, Mateo 10:30)

English

God, our Heavenly Father, loves his children and I am one of them! The Lord my God has chosen me to be his own special treasure. God knew me before he formed me in my mother's womb. Before I was born, God set me apart and appointed me. (Deuteronomy 7:6, Jeremiah 1:5b, NLT)

Spanish

Dios, nuestro Padre celestial, ama a sus hijos y yo soy uno de ellos! Porque ustedes son un pueblo apartado especialmente para el Señor su Dios; el Señor los ha elegido de entre todos los pueblos de la tierra, para que ustedes le sean un pueblo especial. Antes de darte la vida, ya te había yo escogido; antes de que nacieras, ya te había yo apartado; te había destinado a ser profeta de las naciones. (Deuteronomio 7:6, Jeremías 1:5)

English

But I am not alone as God's child! I am a part of a chosen generation, a royal priesthood, a holy nation, a peculiar people! We are the body of Christ, and each one of us is a part of it! (1 Peter 2:9, KJV)

Spanish

Pero no estoy sola como hija de Dios! Soy parte de una familia escogida, un sacerdocio al servicio del rey, una nación santa, un pueblo adquirido por Dios! (1 Pedro 2:9) Somos el cuerpo de Cristo y cada uno de nosotros forma parte de él.

English

But there is a thief who wants to steal, kill, and destroy. Jesus' purpose is to give us a rich and satisfying life in the kingdom. Amen! (John 10:10, NLT)

Spanish

Pero hay un ladrón que viene solamente para robar, matar y destruir; pero yo he venido para que tengan vida, y para que la tengan en abundancia. (Juan 10:10)

English

In the kingdom we have sisters and brothers, but God is our father in heaven, and he loves us! God loved the world so much that he gave his one and only Son, so that everyone who believes in him will not perish but have eternal life. (Matthew 6:9, John 3:16; NLT)

Spanish

En el reino, tenemos hermanas y hermanos, pero Dios es nuestro Padre en el cielo y Él nos ama! Pues Dios amó tanto al mundo, que dio a su Hijo único, para que todo aquel que cree en el no muera, sino que tenga vida eterna. (Mateo 6:9, Juan 3:16)

English

God has given each of us a gift to serve one another! I can serve others because I know nothing in all creation will ever be able to separate me from the love of God that is revealed in Christ Jesus. The Lord keeps me from all harm and watches over my life, so nothing gets past my Heavenly Father. (Romans 8:39b, Psalm 121:7, Nʟᴛ)

Spanish

Puedo servir a otros porque sé que nada podrá separarnos del amor que Dios nos ha mostrado en Cristo Jesús nuestro Señor. El Señor te protege de todo peligro; él protege tu vida. (Romanos 8:39, Salmo 121:7)

English

In fact, no weapon turned against me will succeed, and I will silence every voice raised up to accuse me! (Isaiah 54:17a, N<small>LT</small>)

Spanish

De hecho! Nadie ha hecho el arma que pueda destruirte. Dejaras callado a todo el que te acuse. Esto es lo que yo doy a los que me sirven: la victoria. El Señor es quien lo afirma. (Isaías 54:17)

Helmet of Salvation

Shield of Faith

Breastplate of Righteousness

Belt of Truth

Sword of the Spirit

Feet Shod with the Gospel

English

Every day I can put on the whole armor of God, humble myself before God, resist the devil, and he will flee because the Lord is for me! (Ephesians 6:11a, James 4:7, Psalm 118:6a; NLT)

Spanish

Cada día protéjanse con toda la armadura que Dios les ha dado, para que puedan estar firmes contra los engaños del diablo sométanse, pues, a Dios. Resistan al diablo, y éste huirá de ustedes porque el Señor está conmigo; el me ayuda. He de ver derrotados a todos los que me odian! (Efesios 6:11, Santiago 4:7, Salmo 118:6)

English

Because God is with me, my future is bright and I am on my way! God knows the plans he has for me! Plans of good and not for disaster, to give me a future and a hope! (Jeremiah 29:11, N<small>LT</small>)

Spanish

Porque Dios está conmigo, mi futuro es brillante and yo voy encaminada! Yo sé que planes tengo para ustedes, planes para su bienestar y no para su mal, a fin de darles un futuro lleno de esperanza. Yo, el Señor, lo afirmo. (Jeremías 29:11)

www.ingramcontent.com/pod-product-compliance
Lightning Source LLC
Chambersburg PA
CBHW071229130626
46555CB00004B/1914